FREE THROW

Anastasia Suen

illustrated by Sean Tiffany

Librarian Reviewer
Chris Kreie, Media Specialist

Reading Consultant
Mary Evenson, Teacher

www.raintreepublishers.co.uk
Visit our website to find out
more information about
Raintree books.

To order:
☎ Phone 0845 6044371
🖷 Fax +44 (0) 1865 312263
🖳 Email myorders@capstonepub.co.uk

Customers from outside the UK please telephone +44 1865 312262

Raintree is an imprint of Capstone Global Library Limited, a company incorporated in England and Wales having its registered office at 7 Pilgrim Street, London, EC4V 6LB – Registered company number: 6695582

"Raintree" is a registered trademark of Pearson Education Limited, under licence to Capstone Global Library Limited

Text © Stone Arch Books, 2007
First published in the United Kingdom
by Capstone Global Library in 2010
The moral rights of the proprietor have been asserted.

Edited in the UK by Catherine Veitch
Art Director: Heather Kindseth
Cover Graphic Designer: Heather Kindseth
Interior Graphic Designer: Kay Fraser
Originated by Capstone Global Library
Printed and bound in China by Leo Paper Products Ltd

ISBN 978 1 406213 78 2 (hardback)
14 13 12 11 10
10 9 8 7 6 5 4 3 2 1

ISBN 978 1 406213 99 7 (paperback)
14 13 12 11 10
10 9 8 7 6 5 4 3 2 1

British Library Cataloguing in Publication Data
Suen, Anastasia.
Free throw. -- (Sport stories)
813.6-dc22
A full catalogue record for this book is available from the British Library.

Disclaimer
All the Internet addresses (URLs) given in this book were valid at the time of going to press. However, due to the dynamic nature of the Internet, some addresses may have changed, or sites may have changed or ceased to exist since publication. While the author and publishers regret any inconvenience this may cause readers, no responsibility for any such changes can be accepted by either the author or the publishers.

Contents

Chapter 1

THEO CHAMBERS, CENTRE

Theo watched as people came into the gym and sat on the benches. The fans for his team, the Eagles, sat on one side, and the visiting team's fans from Woodham sat on the other side. Theo couldn't wait for the season to start. Last year Jason played as centre, but now Theo was taller than Jason, so Coach Taylor had changed the roster.

Coach Taylor called the team over. "Theo, I want you to do the tip-off."

"Okay, Coach," said Theo.

"But, Coach," said Jason. "I always do the tip-off!"

"Theo is taller than you this year," said Coach Taylor. "That's why I made him the centre and moved you to forward."

"But he's never done it before," said Jason.

"I'm sure Theo can do it," said Coach. Then he looked at each member of the team. "I'm sure you can all do your job. This is the first game of the season for the Eastmoor Eagles," he said. "I know you'll make me proud."

Theo, Jason, and the other players put their hands into the circle. Coach Taylor put his hand on top. Everyone shouted, "Go, Eagles!"

Theo walked out to the centre of the court and waited for the referee to start the game.

Jason walked up to Theo. "You think you're so great," he said.

"What?" said Theo.

"You think you're better than I am," said Jason, "but you're not."

"I never said that!"

"I'll show you who's great and who's not," said Jason. "Just watch your back." Then he turned and walked away.

Great, thought Theo. I grow a few inches, and our star player hates me.

The referee came over with the ball. He looked at Theo and the centre from Woodham. "Ready, boys?"

"Ready," said Theo.

"I'm ready," said the other boy.

"Then let's get this game started," said the referee. He threw the ball up into the air.

Theo jumped up. But the Woodham centre hit the ball before Theo could reach it. Theo watched the ball fly to the other side of the court.

One of the Woodham guards caught it and ran toward the basket.

Jason ran past Theo. "I knew you couldn't do it," said Jason.

"What a way to start a game," thought Theo. He ran towards the basket.

As Theo reached the key, the free throw lane, the Woodham centre was already in the air. How did he move so fast? Theo watched as the ball dropped into the basket. Woodham scored.

Chapter 2

PASSING GAME

The score was 25 to 14, and Woodham were ahead. Coach Taylor had called a time-out, but he didn't seem upset. He was talking to Tom about the next play.

Tom ran back onto the court. The referee handed Tom the ball. Tom took the ball out of bounds behind the basket.

Then he passed the ball to Raj. Theo ran over to the key and turned around. He raised his hands into the air.

Raj passed the ball to Liam. Theo ran up to the low post by the basket.

Liam passed the ball to Jason. Theo put his hands out, ready to catch the ball. Then a Woodham guard stole the ball from Jason. Jason ran after him.

Theo ran to the other side of the court. He didn't want to let Woodham score again.

As he ran towards the basket, the Woodham players passed the ball. It moved closer and closer to the basket.

"I have to hurry," thought Theo. Their centre is already in the low post, just outside the free throw lane. Theo ran towards the basket.

Just in time! One of the Woodham forwards passed the ball to their centre.

The centre started to jump.

Theo jumped too. He waved his arms to block the shot.

Whap!

The ball flew back towards the centre of the court. Tom grabbed the ball and then passed it to Raj.

"I did it! It's ours again!" thought Theo happily. He headed back toward the other basket.

It was the Eagles' turn to score. Raj passed the ball to Liam. Liam dribbled towards the basket.

The Woodham players surrounded Liam, so he did a left fake. Then he passed the ball to Tom.

Tom was on the wing, but the Woodham players were all over him.

Tom faked right and passed to Liam on his left.

The Woodham team ran towards Liam.

Liam pivoted and passed to Jason.

Theo waved his arms at Jason. Jason looked at Theo and shook his head.

"I'm open," thought Theo. "Jason can see that."

But Jason wouldn't pass. He just jumped and shot.

Chapter 3

CATCHING UP

Theo looked at the scoreboard. Woodham was beating Eastmoor, 37 to 35. They were catching up.

It was Woodham's turn to have the ball. One of the Woodham guards threw the ball in. Theo turned around so he could see where the ball was going.

A quick pass. Theo ran closer to the basket. Another pass. The ball was at the centre of the court.

A third pass was made, and now the players from both teams were over by the basket. Theo watched as the Woodham players passed the ball again.

The Woodham player jumped and so did Theo. Theo waved his arms as he defended the basket. Smack! Theo hit the ball away. Raj ran after the ball.

Theo ran past Raj to the other basket. Liam stopped at the centre of the court court. He turned around to face Raj. Raj passed the ball to Liam.

Theo raised his hands. No one is here but me, he thought. Liam turned and looked at Theo. Liam passed the ball to Theo.

Theo caught the ball. Then he turned and jumped.

The ball sailed through the air.

It hit the rim and dropped into the basket. Two points.

Now the score was tied at 37! Theo looked over at Coach Taylor. "Atta boy!" said his coach. Then Theo saw Jason. Jason was frowning. What's the matter with him? Theo thought. Doesn't Jason want us to win?

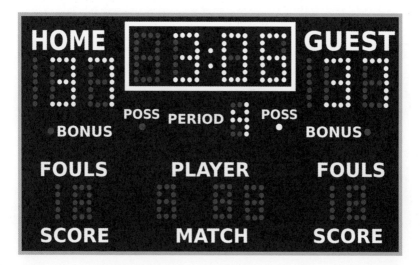

Chapter 4

PERSONAL FOUL

Theo jumped up to block yet another shot, but the Woodham centre faked his jump. Instead he threw the ball to one of the Woodham forwards. Before Theo could reach him, the Woodham forward tipped the ball into the basket. Now the score was 39 to 37.

The referee handed the ball to Tom. Tom stepped out of bounds and looked at the court. Then he threw the ball.

Liam moved in to catch the ball, so Theo ran back across the court. There was only a minute left to play.

Tom dribbled the ball and passed it to Liam. Liam did a fake to the right and passed the ball to Raj on his left.

Theo moved to the low post under the basket. Garret dribbled the ball to the point and looked for an opening. Theo waved his arms. Raj passed him the ball.

At last, thought Theo as he turned towards the basket. Now we can finally tie the game.

Suddenly Theo was sitting on the floor. All he could see was a forest of legs. The referee blew the whistle. "Personal foul," he called.

The Woodham players looked at one another, and then at their coach.

"Did they think that no one would notice?" Theo thought. He picked himself up as Coach Taylor talked to the referee.

Theo walked over to the free throw line. Players from both teams lined up along the lane. The referee handed Theo the ball.

Everyone turned and looked at Theo.

"Don't mess up," said Jason.

Theo looked at Jason. Then he looked at the basket. "I hate free throws," he said to himself. Theo lifted the ball into the air and paused. Then he shot it. The ball hit the rim and bounced out.

The referee threw the ball back to Theo.

"Come on, Theo," said Tom. "We need this point."

"He can't make it," said Jason.

Yes, I can, thought Theo, and he lifted up the ball. Theo studied the basket. Then he threw. The ball landed on the top of the rim. For just a second nobody moved. Then the ball rolled slowly off the rim. No basket. Not again!

Theo ran in to catch the rebound, but the Woodham guard beat him to it. Before Theo could catch him, the Woodham guard scored a basket.

Bzzzt! The buzzer sounded. The game was over!

Jason ran up to Theo. "We lost the game because of you! You're making us all look bad!"

Chapter 5

GAME PLAN

For the next week, Theo practised free throws all the time. He practised over the weekend and after school. "I have to get this right," he told himself.

Theo walked into the gym on the day of the next game. "I am really ready for this game," he thought. Then he saw Jason.

"Why did you bother coming?" said Jason. "We all know you can't play."

Liam looked away. He didn't say anything. "Jason, stop talking rubbish," said Tom.

"Over here, boys," said Coach Taylor. "We have to talk."

Theo waited for the other boys to walk over first. He followed behind them and stood in the back.

"Come on, Theo," said the coach. "I want everyone to hear this." Theo moved into the circle.

"We're playing Portsmouth today," said Coach Taylor. "My old friend Coach O'Reilly is their coach. We played together when we were your age, back when the dinosaurs were alive," said Coach Taylor.

"Dinosaurs?" said Liam.

"Yeah," said their coach, "we used dinosaur eggs instead of basketballs."

"What?" said Tom.

"Just pulling your leg," said Coach Taylor. "Anyway, I want to win this one." He looked around at all the players.

Jason looked at Theo. Then he looked back at the coach.

"We'll do our best," said Tom.

"That's all I ask," said the coach. He took out his notebook.

"Theo, I want you to do the tip-off again," said Coach Taylor.

"What? But he missed the last one," said Jason.

"Give him time," said Coach Taylor.

"But I never miss," said Jason.

"Let's go over our tactics," said Coach Taylor. "I want to use the two-three zone defence. Theo, you're the tallest, so stay right under the basket."

"Okay, Coach," said Theo.

"I play that spot," said Jason.

Coach Taylor looked at Jason, "You're the second tallest, Jason," said Coach, "so I want you in the corner on the right."

"The corner?" asked Jason.

"Yes. And you, Liam," said Coach Taylor, "protect the left corner."

"Will do," said Liam.

"And you two guards," said the coach, "you'll stay between the point and the wing. Raj, you play the right side."

"I'll take the left," said Tom.

"Now, let's get out there and show my old mate who's got the better team!" said Coach Taylor, with a big smile.

Chapter 6

SHOWTIME!

Coach Taylor put his hand into the middle of the team huddle.

All the other players put their hands in and shouted, "Go, Eagles!"

Then the referee walked to the centre of the court. "It's time," said Coach Taylor. "Let's show them how the Eagles fly!"

"Yeah," said Jason, and he punched his fist into the air.

Theo walked out to centre court to do the tip-off.

The referee looked at Theo and at the centre from Portsmouth.

"Are you ready to play?" he asked.

Theo nodded. "Ready," he said.

"Yeah," said the Portsmouth centre.

"Here goes nothing," thought Theo. The referee threw the ball up into the air. Theo jumped as high as he could.

But the centre from Portsmouth hit the ball away. Not again!

Theo ran to the other side of the court. "I told the coach you couldn't do it," said Jason, as he ran by. Theo ignored Jason and kept running. He had to get under the basket!

"Defence!" yelled Coach Taylor. "Defend your zones!"

Theo ran into position under the basket. The Portsmouth players passed the ball left, then right. Theo watched the players weave in and out. Block it, Tom! Block it, Raj!

But the ball came closer and closer.

Then one of the Portsmouth guards passed the ball to their centre.

Here we go, thought Theo. He watched as Jason moved right to try and block the Portsmouth centre. The Portsmouth centre faked right and then jumped left. He shot the ball towards the net.

Theo reached up and jumped as high as he could. It's up to me now.

The ball sailed over Theo's hands.

Swoosh! The ball landed in the net.

Two points already!

The referee gave Tom the ball. Tom went out of bounds and everyone ran into position.

Tom passed the ball to Raj. Raj dribbled the ball to the centre of the court.

Theo ran into the key. He was ready.

But the Portsmouth centre stood between Theo and Raj, so Raj passed the ball to Dylan.

Dylan faked left, and the Portsmouth centre moved towards him. Suddenly Theo was open.

Theo reached out, and Dylan passed him the ball.

Chapter 7

DEFENCE

Theo jumped up to shoot the ball. The Portsmouth centre turned and hit Theo's arm. The ball fell to the ground.

Tweeet! The referee blew his whistle. "Personal foul."

Theo walked to the free throw line. Tom came over to talk.

"You have to make these free throws," said Tom. "We need the points."

"I know, I know," said Theo. "I'll do my best."

The players lined up along the free throw lane. The referee handed Theo the ball. Theo stared at the basket. He tried to ignore Jason. "I can't let him make me miss," he thought to himself.

Theo lifted his arms and shot. Thwack! The ball hit the rim and dropped out.

"Not again," said Jason.

The ref handed Theo the ball. One more try.

Theo lifted the ball. I have to make this one! He pushed his arms up. But the ball bounced off the backboard.

One of the Portsmouth guards caught it. He passed it to another Portsmouth guard.

The players all turned and started moving towards the other basket.

"I don't know why Coach taylor made you centre," said Jason as he passed Theo. "Just because you're tall doesn't mean you're any good!"

"Defence," yelled Coach from the sidelines. Theo turned and ran towards the other basket. "I have to defend my zone!" he thought.

Before Theo could reach the key, the other side had scored!

Jason ran back to Theo.

"Where were you? You're supposed to be under their basket when they have the ball!" he yelled.

Theo looked at Jason. "Sorry."

"Sorry doesn't cut it," said Jason. "We're here to win, not apologize."

"Look alive," said Coach Taylor.

Theo turned and saw that Tom had taken the ball out of bounds. Theo ran back to the centre of the court to get ready.

Chapter 8

FAST PACE

The team from Portsmouth loved the fast pace. Theo ran up and down across the court more times than he could count. By the last quarter, the score was 70 to 69, with Portsmouth in the lead.

Coach Taylor called a time-out. "We have less than a minute left," he said. "We only need one basket to win."

"We won't let you down, Coach," said Tom. He put his hand into the circle.

Coach put his hand in, so Theo did too. Liam, Raj, and Jason put in their hands. Jason's hand was on top. "Go, Eagles," they all yelled. And then the Eagles walked out onto the court.

The referee handed Tom the ball. Tom walked out of bounds with it and turned around slowly.

Theo ran to midcourt. "We need to get this right!" he told himself.

Tom passed the ball to Liam. Liam pivoted and passed the ball to Raj. Theo ran under the basket.

Tom ran into the key. Raj passed Tom the ball, but the players from Portsmouth were all over him. Tom did a fake and passed to Dylan. Dylan moved onto the wing.

Theo put his hands up to catch the ball, but Jason ran in front of him. Dylan passed the ball to Jason instead. Jason turned around, so Theo put his hands out to catch the ball. Jason shook his head. Then he jumped up to shoot.

The Portsmouth centre jumped too, and just as Jason took the shot, the centre hit the ball away.

"Why didn't Jason pass me the ball?" thought Theo angrily. "I was right under the basket."

One of the Portsmouth forwards grabbed the ball. Everyone ran to the other end of the court. Time was running out.

Theo ran as fast as he could to the other basket. "I have to block this!"

He jumped up, and wham! He hit the ball away.

"Attaboy, Theo!" yelled Coach Taylor from the sidelines.

Tom grabbed the ball, and the race was on. Everyone ran back to the other end of the court. Theo ran back to the basket and waited.

Tom passed to Raj. Raj passed to Dylan. Dylan passed to Liam. Then Liam pivoted and passed the ball to Theo.

"At last," thought Theo, and he jumped with the ball. But an arm came out of nowhere and pushed Theo.

The referee's whistle blew. "Personal foul."

"Oh no," thought Theo. "I have to make a free throw again!"

Chapter 9

FREE THROW

Theo walked to the free throw line. Players from both teams lined up on the free throw lane.

"The game's in your hands, Theo," said Tom. "If you make both of these shots, we win."

The referee handed Theo the ball.

"Everyone is watching me," thought Theo. He lifted the ball and eyed the basket.

"You're going to miss!" someone yelled from the benches.

Theo shot the ball. It sailed through the air and hit the backboard. Then it bounced off the rim and fell to the ground. "I hate free throws!" he thought.

Theo looked over at Coach Taylor. The coach touched his knee.

"My knees," thought Theo. "I forgot to bend my knees when I threw."

The referee handed Theo the ball. This is my last try, thought Theo. If I make this, we can tie it up. Theo lifted the ball, bent his knees, and shot.

The ball sailed though the air.

It hit the front of the rim and bounced off. A forward from Portsmouth grabbed the ball. The buzzer sounded.

"We lost," thought Theo. "We lost again because of me!" Jason ran up to Theo. "Don't you ever practise?"

"The game's over," said Tom.

"Theo's over too," said Jason. "Coach Taylor will have to take him off the team now. He can't keep a player who makes the team lose every week."

"Boys," said the coach, "what's done is done. Coach O'Reilly's team beat us. It happens. But don't worry about it. We'll come back."

"But, Coach," said Jason, "we have a losing record."

"The season's not over yet," said Coach Taylor. "We have plenty of time to win."

Coach Taylor looked at Theo.

"Son," he said, "I think we need to move you back to a forward postion for a while. Jason can play centre for a few weeks while you work on your free throws."

"That's fine with me," said Jason. "We did that last year and we had a winning record."

"Yes, we did," said Coach. "And we will again. It just takes a little practise."

Jason patted Theo on the shoulder. "Just practise those free throws, mate, and you can be as good as me."

"I'm going to practise all right," thought Theo. "I'll keep practising until I'm *better* than you!"

Chapter 10

EASTMOOR VS. CHESTER

The next week, as he walked into the gym, Theo thought, "Here we go. My first game this season as a forward, now that Jason has got his way."

"Hi, Theo," said Coach Taylor. "Have you been practising your free throws? Remembering to bend your knees?"

"Yeah," said Theo. "See?" Theo picked up a ball and went over to the free throw line.

He lifted the ball, bent his knees, and shot carefully.

The ball sailed right into the basket.

"That looks great!" said Coach Taylor.

"Thanks," said Theo.

He turned around and saw Jason walk in with Liam.

"The Eagle's centre has arrived," said Jason. He lifted his arms and looked at the benches as if he were a rock star.

"The Eagle's centre was already here," thought Theo. "Just you wait, Jason. I'll get my position back."

"Time to warm up, boys," said the coach.

The Eagles went through some drills as the team from Chester arrived.

"That was a good warm-up, boys," said Coach Taylor. "Now come over here so we can talk about defence."

Theo walked back to the Eagles bench. Jason shot one more basket before he came over.

"Show-off." thought Theo.

"I'm glad you could join us," said Coach Taylor as Jason joined the huddle.

"Sure," said Jason.

"Let's get down to business," said Coach Taylor. He showed them his clipboard. "I want to try the one-two-two defence this week. Theo, you defend the point." Theo nodded.

"Guards, you two stand at the top of the key."

"Yes, sir," said Tom.

"Got it," said Raj.

"Jason and Liam, I want you two in the low post. If all the other defenses fail, it's your job to keep the other team from scoring."

"Okay," said Liam. Jason nodded.

Coach Taylor turned around. "We're ready for the tip-off. Jason, you're playing centre, so it's up to you."

"I can handle it," said Jason, "unlike some people we know," he added.

"What was that?" said Coach Taylor.

"I'm ready to start," said Jason.

"Great," thought Theo. "Go Eagles."

Chapter 11

THE GIANT

"The point. I'm defending the point," Theo said to himself as he walked onto the court. "I hope I remember to stay there!" he thought.

Theo looked at Jason in centre court. "I should be doing the tip-off," he thought sadly.

Then Theo saw the centre from Chester. What a giant! The boy was at least five inches taller than Jason.

The referee threw the ball into the air and the game began. Theo watched as Jason jumped up. But the giant was too tall for Jason. He slapped the ball away.

"Yes," thought Theo. "Jason didn't do it."

Theo turned. The ball was coming right at him. He put up his hands and caught the ball.

The giant ran towards him. Theo passed the ball to Tom, then he ran towards the basket.

"What are you doing here?" said Jason as Theo ran under the basket. "I'm playing centre now."

"Uh, sorry," said Theo, and he moved back to the centre of the lane.

"Pay attention!" said Jason.

Theo turned and Liam passed him the ball. Theo jumped and shot the ball towards the basket. It went right in!

"Two points," thought Theo. "I scored the first two points of the game!"

"Why didn't you pass it to me?" said Jason, who was running to the other side of the court.

"Why should I?" thought Theo. "You're not the only player on our team."

Theo ran to the point and guarded his spot. He watched Jason run over to the low post. The giant jumped up, and bam! Two points! Jason wasn't tall enough to block him.

Tom took the ball out and everyone scrambled. Theo ran back into the key.

Jason ran past him.

"Can't you do anything right?" said Jason. "This is my area now. Go out and get the ball."

"You bet I will," thought Theo. As he moved towards the centre of the court, Theo saw Liam catch the ball. Liam pivoted. He did a fake to the left and then threw the ball right to Theo!

Theo caught the ball. He turned and jumped. Off the ball flew. Bam! Right into the basket.

"Yes! I did it again!"

"Attaboy!" yelled Coach Taylor.

Jason came over with a scowl on his face. "I'm the centre. Pass it to me."

Chapter 12

SURPRISE!

Theo scored.

The giant scored.

Theo scored.

The giant scored.

The fourth quarter was almost over and the score was 53 to 51, to Chester.

Coach Taylor called a time-out. "Jason, you have to stop their centre from scoring."

"I'm trying, Coach," said Jason, "but he's a giant."

"I can see that," said Coach Taylor. "But you still have to guard him." Coach looked at his clipboard. "I think it's time for someone else to play centre."

"But, Coach!" said Jason.

"If you can't do the job," said Coach, "then we need to give it to someone else. We're zero and two this season."

"Because of Theo," said Jason.

"Theo has scored most of our points this game," said Coach Taylor.

"He never passes to me," said Jason.

"Their centre has you blocked," said Coach. "It's not about you, Jason. It's what's best for the team."

"I know," said Jason, "but—"

"No buts about it," said Coach. He turned to Theo. "I want you to play centre for the rest of the game, Theo. Jason, you go back to forward."

"Theo?" asked Jason.

"Okay, Coach," said Theo.

"It's the element of surprise," said Coach Taylor. "They won't be expecting us to move our top scorer to a new position so late in the game."

Jason gave Theo a dirty look.

"We're only down by two points," said Coach Taylor. "Let's win this one!"

The giant had just scored, so the ball went to Eastmoor.

Tom took the ball out.

Theo ran back towards the basket. I have my job back! Now I have to show Coach Taylor that I can stay here!

Tom passed the ball to Raj. Raj made a fast pass to Jason. Jason passed the ball to Liam. Liam turned around and jumped! The ball went in the basket. Two points! The score was tied at 53.

Now the giant's team had the ball. Theo ran back to the other basket. I have to keep the giant from scoring.

Just like clockwork, the Chester team passed the ball to the giant. He came up to the low post, and Theo jumped up to block his shot. Whap! The ball flew back to centre court.

"What!" yelled the giant.

"It was a surprise," thought Theo as he ran to the other side of the court. Theo ran to the low post and Raj passed him the ball. Theo jumped up. "Now we can win."

Wham!

Suddenly Theo was flat on his back.

Tweeet! The ref blew the whistle. "Personal foul."

Theo picked himself up off the floor. "Man, that giant can hit!" Thought Theo. Theo's back throbbed as he walked over to the free throw line.

He glanced at the clock. There were only two seconds left in the game!

"You can do it, Theo" said Tom.

Theo rubbed his aching back.

The referee handed him the ball. "You have two throws," he said.

Theo nodded his head. He lifted the ball and studied the basket. Then he bent his knees and shot the ball.

Clank! The first shot hit the rim and bounced out.

I have to make this second one, thought Theo.

The referee handed Theo the ball again. "Last shot."

"Don't I know it," thought Theo. "I have to show Coach that I can shoot free throws!"

Theo lifted the ball and looked at the basket. "Here goes nothing!" He bent his knees and shot the ball.

The ball sailed through the air.

Swish! The ball dropped right into the centre of the net!

Bzzzt! The buzzer rang.

The game was over.

"Game point," thought Theo.

"We won! I did it!"

About the author

Anastasia Suen is the author of more than seventy books for young people. She enjoys watching basketball because the game moves so quickly!

About the illustrator

When Sean Tiffany was growing up, he lived on a small island. Every day, he had to take a boat to get to school. When Sean isn't working on his art, he works on a multimedia project called "OilCan Drive", which combines music and art. He has a pet cactus named Jim.

Glossary

fake false move that tricks an opponent

foul making unfair contact with
another player

free throw throw taken by a player who
has been fouled

huddle a tight grouping of team members

key area in front of the basket

offence when players on a team try to score

pivot to turn suddenly

roster list of players on a team

tactic planned action to win at something

tip-off move that starts a game, where two
players jump for a ball

Cool facts . . .

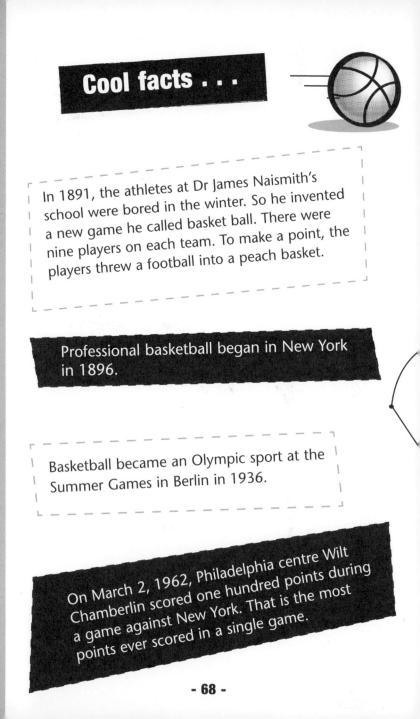

In 1891, the athletes at Dr James Naismith's school were bored in the winter. So he invented a new game he called basket ball. There were nine players on each team. To make a point, the players threw a football into a peach basket.

Professional basketball began in New York in 1896.

Basketball became an Olympic sport at the Summer Games in Berlin in 1936.

On March 2, 1962, Philadelphia centre Wilt Chamberlin scored one hundred points during a game against New York. That is the most points ever scored in a single game.

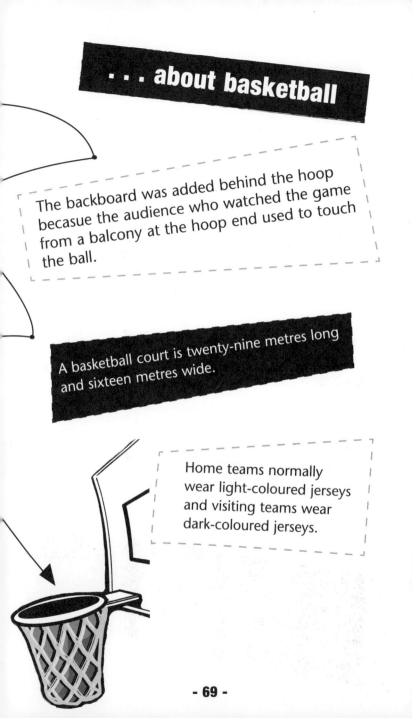

The backboard was added behind the hoop becasue the audience who watched the game from a balcony at the hoop end used to touch the ball.

A basketball court is twenty-nine metres long and sixteen metres wide.

Home teams normally wear light-coloured jerseys and visiting teams wear dark-coloured jerseys.

Discussion questions

1. In the book, the character of Jason is mean to Theo. Do you think it's okay to talk to players on your own team in the way Jason talked to Theo?

2. If you were Theo, what would you have done if the team lost because you missed a free throw?

3. Have you ever played sport with someone like Jason? How would you deal with someone like that?

Writing prompts

1. The main character, Theo, hates doing free throws. Has there ever been something you've had to practise to become better at? If so, write what it was and how you felt after you succeeded.

2. Throughout the game, Theo never tells the coach about Jason and his bad attitude. Do you think this is a good idea or not? Explain.

3. What are some of the reasons the coach kept Theo playing in centre position for so long?

Find out more

Books

Basketball Legends, Mark Woods (ticktock Media, 2009)

How to Improve at Basketball, Andy Horsley (ticktock Media, 2009)

The Sports Book (Dorling Kindersley, 2009)

Sporting Skills: Basketball, Clive Gifford (Wayland, 2008)

Websites

www.british-basketball.co.uk
This is the website for the British Basketball Federation.

www.hoopedia.nba.com
Find out the history of basketball and much more about the game on this useful website by the USA's National Basketball Association.